BLOSSOM TALES
Flower Stories of Many Folk

By Patricia Hruby Powell

Illustrated by Sarah Dillard

Moon Mountain
PUBLISHING

North Kingstown, Rhode Island

To Morgan, who brings our garden to life.
PHP

For my father.
SD

Text Copyright © 2002 Patricia Hruby Powell
Illustrations Copyright © 2002 Sarah Dillard

First edition.

Library of Congress Cataloging-in-Publication Data

Powell, Patricia Hruby, 1951-
     Blossom tales : flower stories of many folk / by Patricia
Hruby Powell ; illustrated by Sarah Dillard.
          p. cm.
     Includes bibliographical references.
     Summary: A collection of fourteen folk tales about
flowers from many different cultures.
     ISBN 0-9677929-8-3 (alk. paper)
     1. Tales. 2. Flowers—Folklore. [1. Flowers—Folklore.
2. Folklore.] I. Dillard, Sarah, 1961- ill. II. Title.

PZ8.1.P8667 B1 2002
398.24'2—dc21

                              2001044833

Moon Mountain Publishing
80 Peachtree Road
North Kingstown, RI 02852
www.moonmountainpub.com

The author thanks the Ragdale Foundation, Lake
Forest, Illinois.

The illustrations in this book were done in gouache on
hot press 140 lb. watercolor paper.

Printed in South Korea

10 9 8 7 6 5 4 3 2 1

CONTENTS

Crocus
Sicily

Nicola walked to the market to sell his family's purple grapes. Whereas the grapes were big and juicy, the boy was small and ragged, and he was ignored in the crowd. By noon he was very hungry, but he knew that if he ate the grapes, his father would punish him. He would wait.

A tattered old woman approached him and said, "Please, could you give me some food?"

She looked even poorer and hungrier than he, so he handed her the best bunch of grapes from his basket. As she ate them, she grew younger and more beautiful, and her shabby clothes turned into a delicate purple gown. The lovely young woman said, "Nicola, take the rest of your grapes home and plant them."

Feeling certain that she was a fairy, Nicola ran home and planted the grapes. As he walked into the house for his punishment, he saw in the basket golden coins, one for each grape the woman had eaten. And for each grape he'd planted in the vineyard, a cluster of purple crocuses bloomed.

Morning Glory
Hawaii

Haumea Papa was a child of the gods.
One day her husband, Wakea, went to hunt
in the Kalihi Valley while Haumea went
fishing in her canoe. Dressed in a blue skirt,
Haumea paddled along sandy beaches and
rocky coasts, but she felt that something was
not right with Wakea. She paddled ashore
and ran through the damp forest until she
saw her husband tied to a tree. The ruling
chief had accused Wakea of poaching and
was going to burn him to death.

Haumea made herself invisible and unbound her husband. Holding hands, the couple entered a great tree right through its bark and into its center. The chief's men tried to cut down the tree but it couldn't be cut. When night came, the men turned away. Haumea and Wakea emerged from the tree and fled through the Kalihi Valley. Brambles and twigs snatched at Haumea's blue skirt and shredded it, but the lovers escaped. The blue tatters from Haumea Papa's skirt bloomed the next morning into a long vine of morning glories all along the path that the lovers had run.

To this day, the flowers open every morning like blue trumpets to welcome the day in the Kalihi Valley. And they close every night, when the sun sets.

Columbine
Iroquois

Long ago, a chief dreamed of Sky Maiden and fell in love. Sky Maiden said, "At the Ring of Five Oaks, I will let down a vine so you may climb into the Skies."

On awakening, the chief searched for the Ring of Five Oaks. He couldn't find it in his own valley. In desperation, he searched the lands of four other chiefs. When he described his dream to them, they too fell in love with Sky Maiden. All five chiefs searched until they found the Ring of Five Oaks on the land of the Fifth Chief. From the center of the ring, a vine stretched into the sky.

First Chief cried, "Sky Maiden's vine!" and began climbing. Second Chief pulled him down. "It's mine!" Third Chief said, "I found it!" All five quarreled. Fourth Chief produced his gambling stones and they sat to cast lots. Great Spirit gazed down at the Five Chiefs huddled in a circle, wearing their crimson shirts and canary-yellow moccasins. He was so angry they would neglect their people that He turned them into the first columbine.

Lily of the Valley
Sussex, England

Saint Leonard met the terrible Dragon, called Sin, on the road. When the beast let out a blast of fire from its nostrils, Leonard pulled out his sword and fought the slimy brute. For three days and three nights the Saint wrestled the monster. On the fourth day, Saint Leonard drove the injured Dragon deep into the forest where it remained dwelling in darkness.

Saint Leonard conquered the Dragon, Sin, but he was wounded by the creature's tearing claws. Where Saint Leonard's blood stained the ground, up sprang the first lilies of the valley. Each little white bell chimed Saint Leonard's victory.

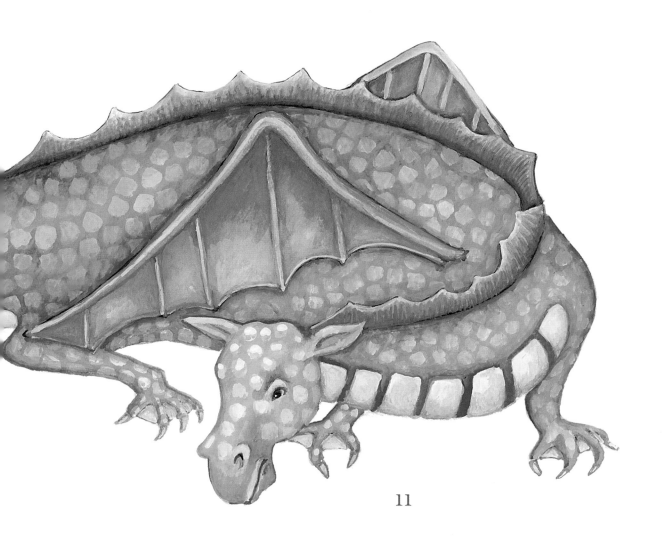

Peony
Japan

A king promised to give his daughter, Princess Aya, to Lord Ako in marriage. One day Aya wandered with her maids through the castle garden, across tiny arched bridges over silver cascades. At the edge of the pond she stooped to breathe in the lovely fragrance of peonies. She slipped, but before she could fall into the water, a handsome youth in a peony-embroidered kimono emerged from the flower bed as if by magic. He caught her, gently set her back on the path, and vanished. Who could he be? The guards had let no one enter. Aya insisted that her maids say nothing to her father of the handsome youth.

Princess Aya would not eat or sleep. She fell ill. The doctors could not help her. Finally one of the maids told her father, the king, of the mysterious youth in the peonies. The king had Aya carried to the garden and entertained by musicians. The music had hardly begun when the youth rose from the peony bed. When the music stopped, he vanished. The guards searched the garden but found no one. On the second night of music the youth appeared and vanished again. On the third night, as the music began, the youth appeared. A waiting guard seized him, uttered a cry, and fainted. Everyone rushed to the collapsed guard. They saw no youth, but in his hand the guard held a bright pink peony.

Princess Aya took the peony to her room where it remained fresh for weeks and weeks. The Princess regained her strength. Bravely, she married Lord Ako. The peony drooped, faded, and died. The story spread, and Aya became known as Princess Peony.

Snapdragon
Russia

A poor woodcutter lived in a hut surrounded by clusters of snapdragons. The yellow, pink and white flowers were the joy of his life. One day in late summer he came home at midday, so that he might be comforted by his glorious snapdragons before the winter frosts came. As he stood in his garden, a dwarf appeared and said, "I'm on a long journey and I'm very hungry."

"I'm a poor man, and I can offer you only dark bread and no butter," said the woodcutter. "But you are welcome to share this meal with me."

"Aha!" said the dwarf. "Let me help you. Good woodcutter, bring the bread." The dwarf quickly filled his cap with snapdragon seeds, and with powerful fingers squeezed them until they oozed oil. He spread the oil on the bread, and the two enjoyed the meal in good fellowship. The dwarf then continued on his journey.

From that day, the woodcutter prospered by making oil from his beautiful snapdragons and selling it in town. And to this day, Russian peasants spread their bread with snapdragon oil.

Nasturtium
Quechua (South America)

The Spanish conquistadors had stolen all the golden idols of the Quechua and melted them down for Spain's treasury. The Quechua needed gold to make new statues of their gods.

One of their people, Quispe, offered to collect the gold. Weaving together branches and grasses, he built a dam across a mountain stream. After the spring floods had rolled down from the top of the mountain, he gathered the gold nuggets trapped by the dam. He gave thanks to the Mountain God by leaving several nuggets on the mountain. He put the rest in a grass bag and walked downhill.

A Spaniard rode his horse uphill. He saw Quispe with his bag of gold and wanted it for Spain. He clubbed Quispe to get his gold.

As Quispe fell to the ground, he implored the Mountain God, "Take the gold back where it came from. Don't let the Spaniard take our gold."

The Mountain God heard Quispe's plea. The Spaniard's horse shied, throwing the rider and the bag of gold. The Spaniard groped through the underbrush, trying to gather the scattered nuggets. But poisonous snakes bit his hands and he died. The gold nuggets from deep within the mountain became luminous gold-yellow flowers, the first nasturtiums scattered across the mountain greenery.

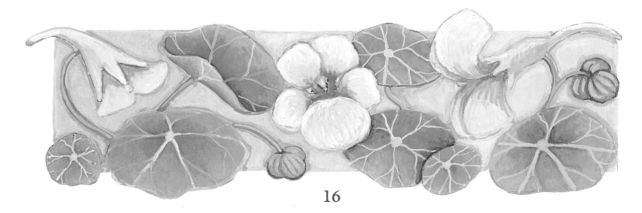

Rose
Persia (Iran)

The Nightingale loved the Rose. Every night he would sing from his heart, and the Rose would open her petals. The other birds felt their peace was disturbed and asked for the judgment of King Solomon.

"All night he sings his mournful song and we cannot sleep," the birds complained.

The Nightingale answered, "But I love the Rose. She waits for my call to open from the bud. I must help her to unfold her perfect beauty."

Wise King Solomon acquitted the Nightingale, and still we hear the Nightingale's song on a still summer night. In the land of Persia, the Rose cannot open her bud without his call.

Dandelion
Ojibwa

One spring day Shawondasee, the South Wind, saw a beautiful slim maiden at a distance. He sighed heavily. She stood amidst the tall grasses, dressed in green, her hair the color of sunshine. Shawondasee whispered, "Tomorrow I will seek the maiden and make her my bride." But the South Wind felt heavy and drowsy as he sat in the shade of flowering trees. The next day he saw her again and vowed to make her his bride. But he was lazy with the perfume of blossoms and closed his sleepy eyes. And so it went.

He looked at her one morning and her golden hair had turned pure white like thistledown. "Ah, my brother the North Wind, with his cruel hand, turned her hair white with frost." Shawondasee heaved such a mighty sigh that his breath reached her and blew off her white hair, scattering it through the air. The maiden was gone.

Now every spring Shawondasee sighs and sighs, longing for the maiden as he first saw her, with hair the color of sunshine.

Alyssum
Italy

One night a man was returning home from a feast in a distant village where he had sung and danced and drunk plenty of wine. Normally he would have taken the open road and avoided the forest, but he was in a hurry. The wine made him so brave he was willing to risk ghosts and the Devil himself in the dark woods. But he brought a sturdy club, just in case.

He had not gone far when he saw a rabbit and thought it would be a perfect dinner. As he chased it, wielding his club, the rabbit became a wolf. The man knew that this was the Devil. He dropped the club and fled. The wolf pursued him. It sprang. In mid-flight it became a wild boar. The man screamed as he ran toward the open meadow, uttering a desperate prayer. He fell weeping into the tufted grass.

No animal was upon him. He smelled a delicious perfume. The man's prayer had turned the grass to sweet alyssum and made the Devil disappear. In Italy the Devil still flees from alyssum, so people hang it in their homes.

23

Mignonette
Egypt

Horus, the god with a falcon's head, looked down from the sky and saw a young woman weeping. He floated down in a cloud and said to her, "Why are you crying?"

The woman could see only the mist off the Red Sea and hear the rumbling voice of the cloud, and she was frightened. She tried to run, but she felt heavy as if in a dream.

"Wait," said the voice in the cloud. "I see your young husband is dead. But Osiris has not yet taken him to the underworld. Take this and bring it to your husband." The cloud rose, and in its place a new flower grew. Its scent was so sweet it made the woman drunk. She picked the flower and ran home to where her husband lay. Before she could find a vase, the perfume of the flower filled the room, and her husband breathed and awoke.

Because of Horus' gift, the mignonette, the young man did not journey with Osiris to the underworld for many a year.

Aster and Goldenrod
Cherokee

Two little girls awakened
to the war cries of an attacking
tribe. They grabbed their
clothes and ran from their log
hut. Deep in the woods they
hid in the hollow tree where
they often played. All day and
all night they huddled together,
crying softly. They knew no one
would be left in their village.

The next day was quiet. They walked through the woods, clinging to each other, wandering up and down hills and wading across creeks, until they came to the hut of an old Herb Woman. The old woman looked at the sisters in their doeskin dresses, one in violet-blue, the other in deeply fringed yellow. She knew the girls were not safe and that the enemy would hunt them down. That night, as the girls slept under the stars, the Herb Woman covered them with leaves and sprinkled a magic potion over them. In the morning the girls had disappeared, but in their place were two flowers. One was like a violet-blue star and the other a yellow plume.

Even today, you'll find aster and goldenrod side by side.

Geranium
Arab

The prophet Mohammed was traveling through the desert, gathering his people together to teach them about Allah. After a long, hot and dusty day, he stopped at a stream to bathe. He washed his linen shirt. Then he climbed up the bank and spread his shirt to dry on a common lavender mallow plant.

While the prophet slept, the mallow plant blushed to think it was honored with the shirt of Allah's holy messenger.

Mohammed awoke refreshed. When he took his shirt from the mallow bush, brilliant red blossoms, exhaling a spicy aroma, bloomed on the plant. The common mallow plant became the first geranium.

Tulip
Devon, England

A kind old woman lived in a thatched hut surrounded by brown tulips, for that was the color of tulips in days long ago. Each autumn Granny planted more tulip bulbs, and each spring she weeded and watered and sang to them. While singing a soft lullaby one moonlit night, she was joined by a chorus of tinkling voices. Peering closely, she saw that tiny fairies fluttered among the tulips, and inside each blossom a baby fairy was cradled.

A pink fairy with a silvery voice sang up to Granny, "You have given us cradles for our babies. Thank you. For that, we will paint your tulips." And the fairy danced away on fluttering wings.

Granny thought it was a dream, but the next morning there were no brown tulips at all. They were all blushing pinks, ruby reds, and buttery yellows. Shortly after, the happy Granny died peacefully, and the fairies planted more colorful tulips and tended her grave.

If you are in a tulip garden at night, you may not see the fairies. If you listen closely, though, you can still hear them singing their babies to sleep as they rock them in their cradles, thanks to Granny's care all those years ago.

Bibliography

Bailey, Carolyn. *For The Children's Hour*. NY: Platt & Munk, [c. 1943].

Beals, Katharine. *Flower Lore and Legend*. NY: Holt, 1917.

Beckwith, Martha Warren. *Hawaiian Mythology*. Honolulu: University of Hawaii, 1970.

Brown, Charles E. *Flower Lore*. Madison, 1938.

Calvino, Italo. *Italian Folktales*. NY: Harcourt, 1980.

Carey, M.C. *Flower Legends*. London: Pearson, 1921.

Cathon, Laura E. *Perhaps and Perchance: Tales of Nature*. NY: Abingdon Press, 1962.

Clouston, William Alexander. *Flowers From A Persian Garden and Other Papers*. NY: Arno, 1977.

Deas, Lizzie. *Flower Favourites*. London: George Allen, 1898.

Farmer, Florence Virginia. *Nature Myths of Many Lands*. NY: American, 1910.

Fox, Frances Margaret. *Flowers And Their Travels*. Indianapolis: Bobbs-Merril, 1936.

Friend, Hilderic. *Flowers and Flower Lore*. London: Sonnenschein, 1886.

Funk & Wagnalls Standard Dictionary of Folklore, Mythology and Legend. ed. by Maria Leach, NY: Funk & Wagnalls, 1949.

Gubernatis, Angelo de. *La Mythologie des Plantes*. Paris: Reinwald, 1882.

Lum, Elizabeth M. *Ancient Legends of Different Nations*. New Haven: Tuttle, 1902.

McFee, Inez N. *A Treasury of Flower Stories*. NY: Crowell, 1921.

Nash, Elizabeth Todd. *101 Legends of Flowers*. Boston: Christopher, 1927.

Olcott, Frances Jenkins. *Wonder Garden*. Boston: Houghton Mifflin, 1919.

Quinn, Vernon. *Stories & Legends of Garden Flowers*. NY: Stokes, 1939.

Singleton, Esther. *The Wildflower Fairy Book*. NY: Dodd, Mead, 1905.

Skinner, Ada. *The Turquoise Story Book*. NY: Duffield, 1918.

Skinner, Charles. *Myths and Legends of Flowers, Trees, Fruits, and Plants*. Philadelphia: Lippincott, 1911.

Stewart, Mary. *Tell Me a Story I Never Heard Before*. NY: Revell, 1919.

Temple, Major Sir Grenville T. *Excursions in the Mediterranean*. London: Saunders, 1835.